Text copyright © 2002 by Kate Banks

Pictures copyright © 2002 by Tomek Bogacki

All rights reserved

Distributed in Canada by Douglas & McIntyre Ltd.

Color separations by Hong Kong Scanner Arts

Printed and bound in the United States of America by Berryville Graphics

Art direction and design by Monika Keano

First edition, 2002

10 9 8 7 6 5 4 3 2 1

Library of Congress Cataloging-in-Publication Data

Banks, Kate, 1960–

    The turtle and the hippopotamus / Kate Banks; pictures by Tomek Bogacki.— 1st ed.

      p. cm.

    Summary: Afraid to cross the river because of the hippopotamus there, a turtle takes

inspiration from other animals in trying other ways to get across.

    ISBN 0-374-37885-1

    [1. Turtles—Fiction.   2. Hippopotamus—Fiction.   3. Animals—Fiction.] I. Bogacki,

Tomasz, ill. II. Title.

PZ7.B22594 Tu 2002

[E]—dc21

                         00-53548

A
REBUS
BOOK

Designed by Monika Keano

KATE BANKS

PICTURES BY TOMEK BOGACKI

THE TURTLE
AND
THE HIPPOPOTAMUS

FRANCES FOSTER BOOKS

FARRAR STRAUS GIROUX

NEW YORK

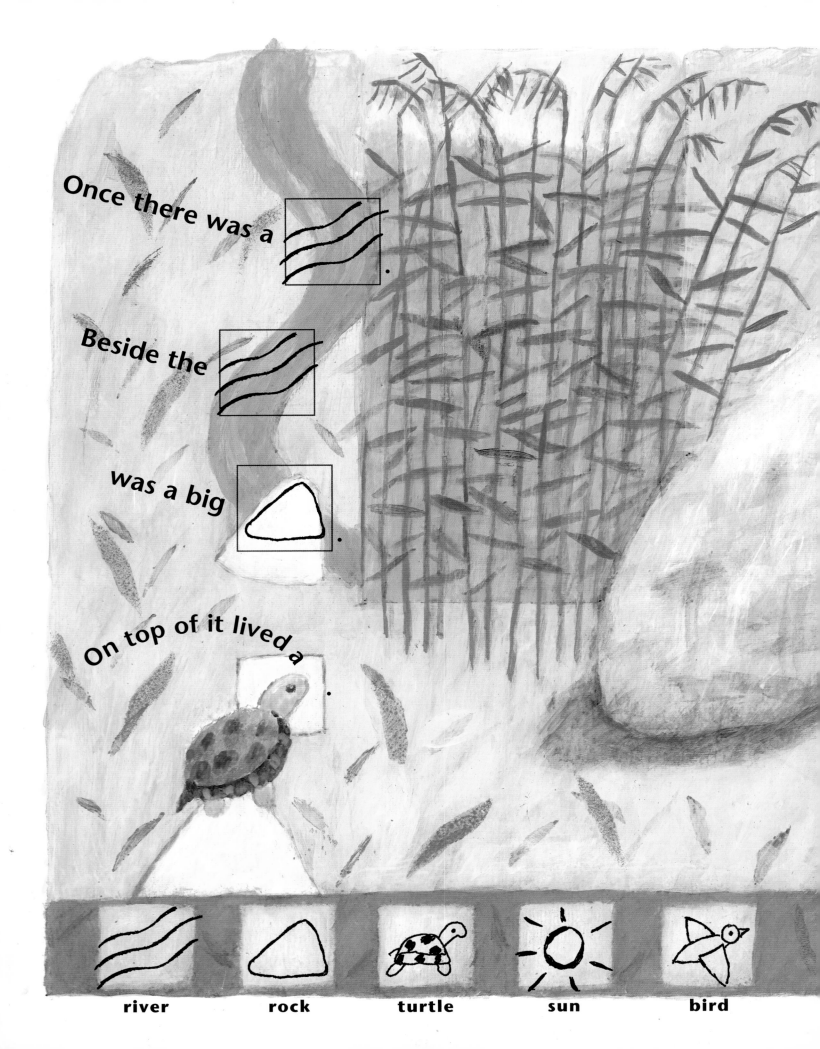

Once there was a [river] .

Beside the [river]

was a big [rock] .

On top of it lived a [turtle] .

river   rock   turtle   sun   bird

The passed each day basking in the , listening to a sing, and eating the that grew along the .

reeds

One day there were no more  left.

"What shall I do?" asked the .

"Swim across the ," said the .

reeds turtle river bird water lilies

On the other side of the  there were tall luscious  and beautiful  .

But in the middle of the  was an enormous

The  was afraid of the  and would not swim across the  .

hippopotamus

So the ⬜ sat back on the ⬜, feeling hungry. She gazed up at the ⬜ that flew across the ⬜.

"If only I had ⬜ like you," she said, "I could fly across the ⬜."

The ⬜ found a torn ⬜ in a nearby ⬜. She mended it with ⬜.

turtle   **rock**   **bird**   **sky**   **wings**

Then she took hold of the
and tried to fly.

river   kite   field   pine needles

But the  could not hold the  and the  tumbled into a patch of prickly .

Beside the prickly  was a  talking to a .

kite   turtle   moss   grasshopper   fly

"Excuse me," said the . "I was just trying to cross the ."

"Why not swim?" said the .

But the  would not swim past the .

river   hippopotamus

The [turtle] looked at the [legs] of the [grasshopper] and sighed.

"If only I could hop across the [river] like you," she said.

turtle   legs   grasshopper   river   tire

Beside the ⬜ was an old rubber ⬜.

The ⬜ tried jumping on the ⬜.

But she toppled off
and landed in a clump of 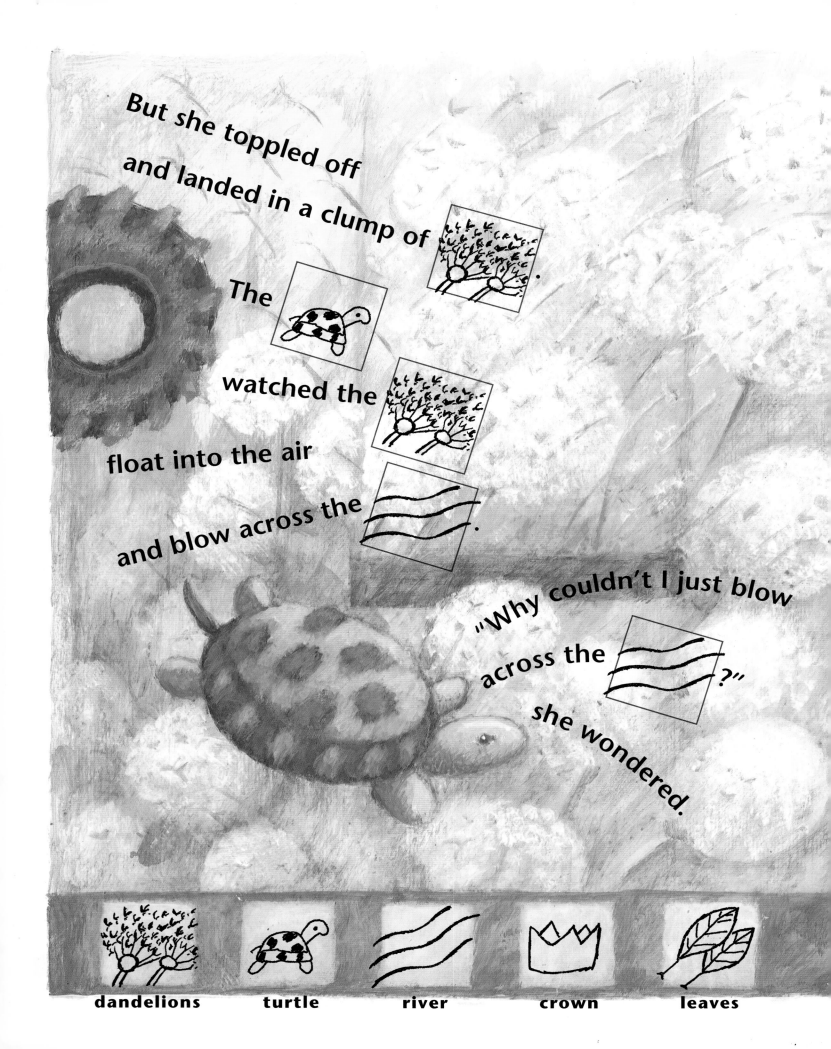 .

The [turtle] watched the [dandelions]

float into the air

and blow across the [river] .

"Why couldn't I just blow across the [river] ?"

she wondered.

dandelions   turtle   river   crown   leaves

The  decorated herself with a  of  and perched herself on the  .

rock

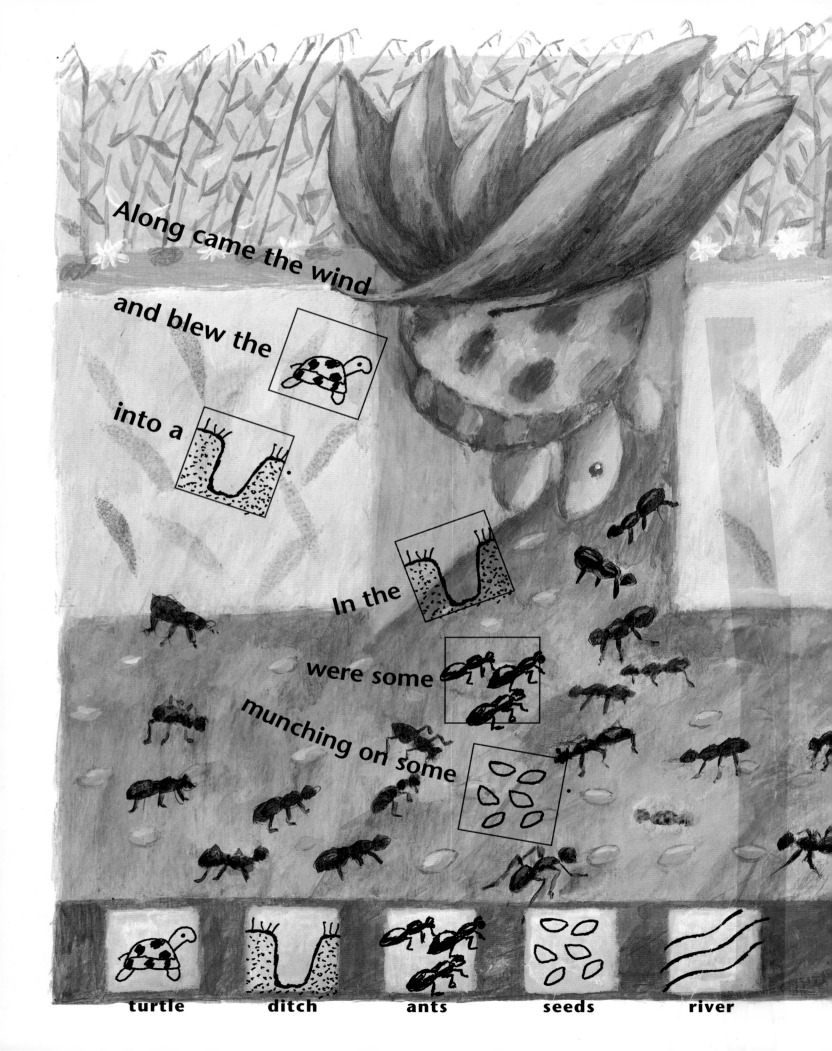

Along came the wind and blew the 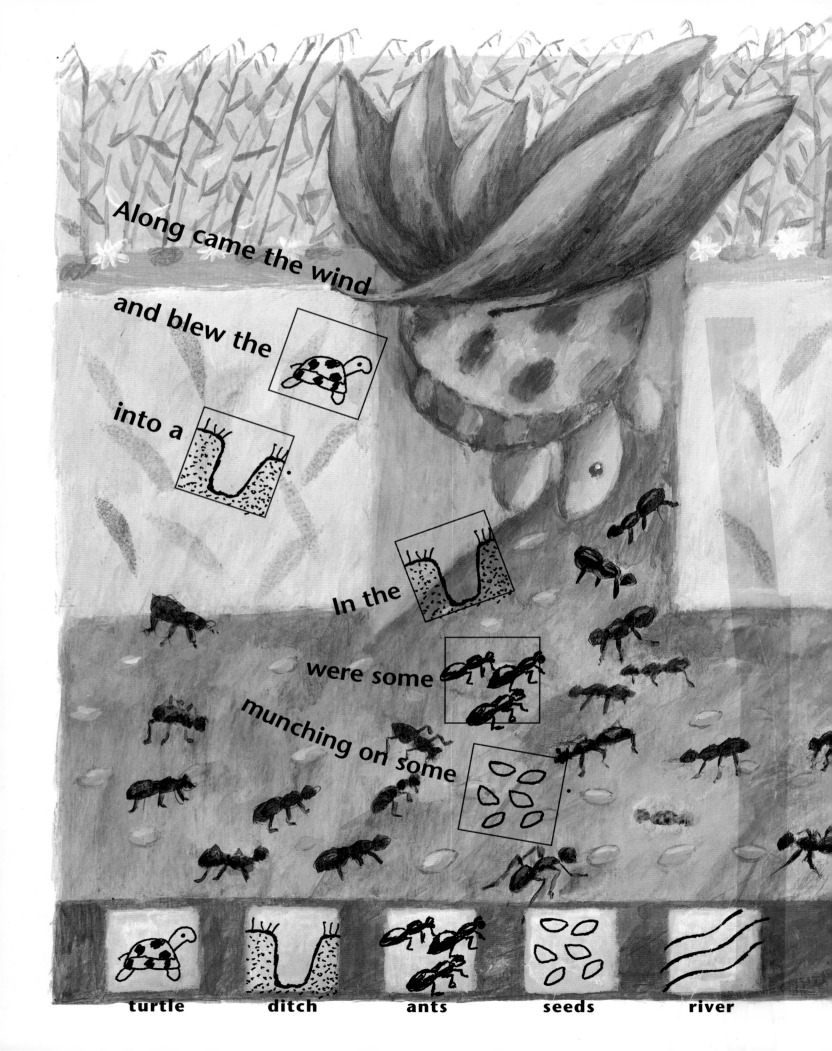 into a .

In the were some munching on some

turtle　　**ditch**　　**ants**　　**seeds**　　**river**

"Sorry," said the 🐢.

"I was just trying to cross the 〰️."

"What about swimming?" sang the 🐜.

But the 🐢 was too afraid of the 🦛 to swim across the 〰️.

hippopotamus

The 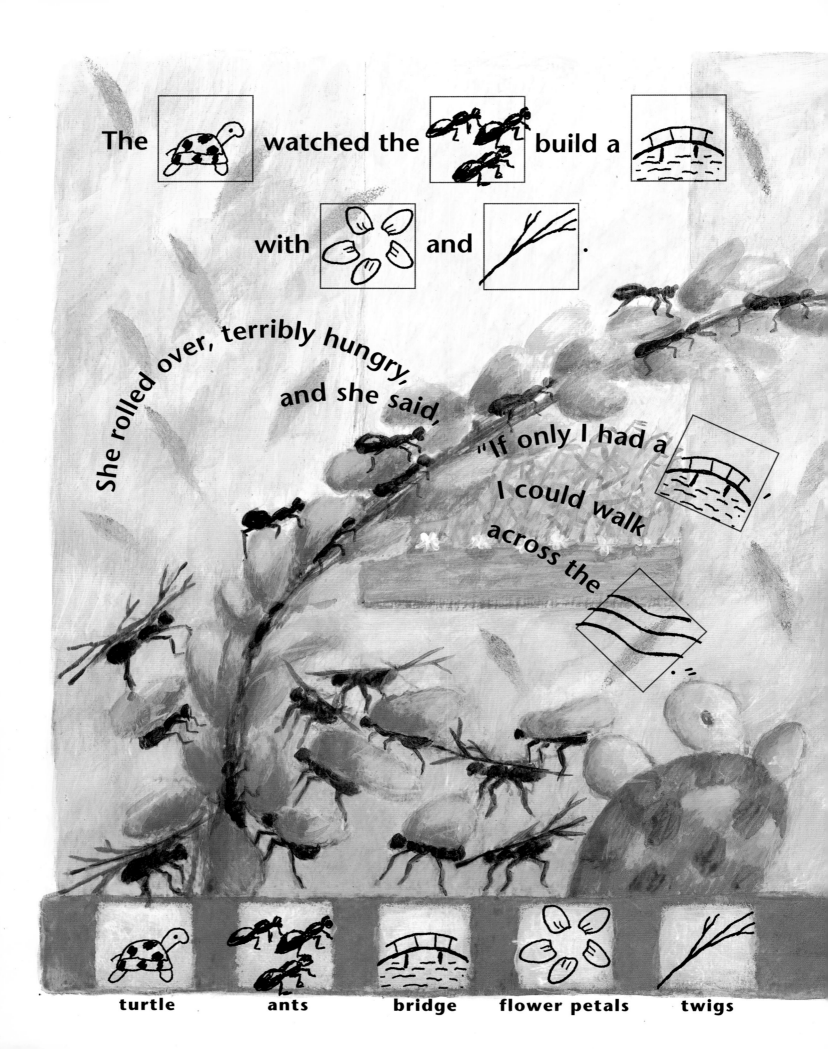 watched the build a

with and .

She rolled over, terribly hungry, and she said, "If only I had a I could walk across the

turtle   ants   bridge   flower petals   twigs

So the  got some , and some ,

and began building a .

river   stones   logs

But the 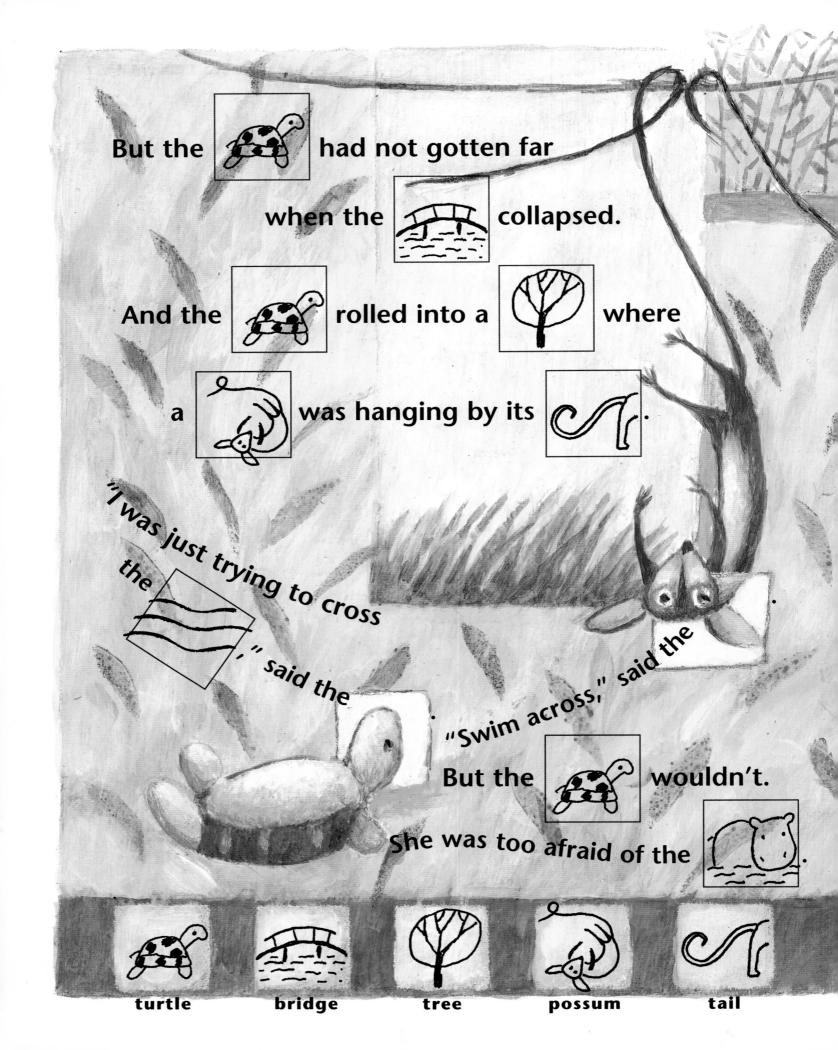 had not gotten far

when the collapsed.

And the rolled into a where

a was hanging by its .

"I was just trying to cross the ," said the .

"Swim across," said the .

But the wouldn't.

She was too afraid of the .

turtle   **bridge**   **tree**   **possum**   **tail**

She watched the  swing back and forth.

"If only I had a  like you, I could swing across the ," she said.

The  looked around and spotted a  hanging from a .

river   hippopotamus   rope   branch

She grabbed hold of the  and swung out over the ⬚ .

But the 🪢 broke, and down went the 🐢 right onto the back of the 🦛 .

"Excuse me," cried the 🐢. "I was just trying to cross the 〰️."

rope	**river**	**turtle**	**hippopotamus**	**mouth**

The  opened his big wide .

The  closed her small frightened .

"Why not swim?" said the .

eyes

Then the  carried the to the other side of the .

He stopped to chomp on the .

"Won't you join me?" he said to the .

hippopotamus   turtle   river   reeds

The  and the  spent the rest of the day eating .

turtle

river

And the next time the  had to cross the , she swam.